This book belongs to:

SCOOBY-DOO! ™

Haunted Ski Lodge

By Gail Herman
Illustrated by Duendes del Sur

ADVANCE
PUBLISHERS

Scooby-Doo!

READ & SOLVE

Find These Fun Activities Inside!

Check the inside back cover for fun things to do!

Bonus story-related activity strips throughout the 15 volumes.

Create your own mystery book, *Scooby-Doo The Swamp Witch!*
Color, collect, and staple the coloring pages at the end of the first 12 books in the Scooby-Doo Read & Solve mystery series.

Advance PUBLISHERS

www.advancepublishers.com
Produced by Judy O Productions, Inc.
Designed by SunDried Penguin Design
All rights reserved.
Printed in China

COUNTING MYSTERY

How many striped
scarves appear
in this book?

"Rrrrr!" "Brrrr!" Scooby-Doo and Shaggy
hugged each other to keep warm.

"Like, it's freezing out here," said Shaggy.

"Well, it is winter," said Velma.

"And we are outside, waiting to ski,"
Daphne added.

"And you are eating ice cream," said Fred.

Shaggy grinned. "Well, Scoob, old buddy. Let's get some *hot* dogs then!"
Scooby's teeth chattered. "Rummy!"
"Ski lodge, here we come!" said Shaggy.

"Not so fast!" said Fred. "We came to this mountain to ski.
And that is what we are going to do."

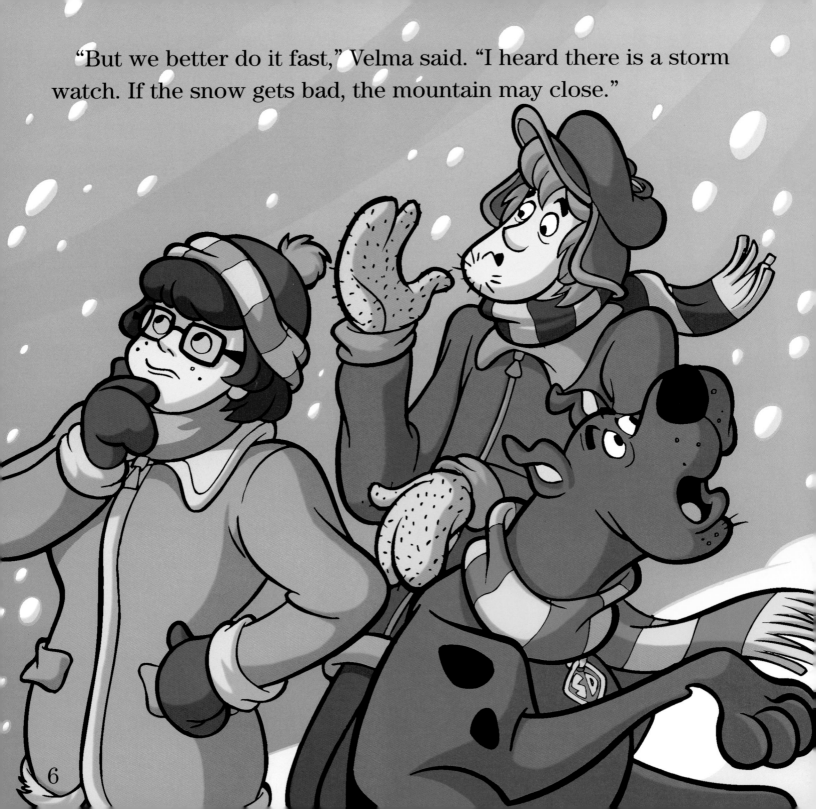

"But we better do it fast," Velma said. "I heard there is a storm watch. If the snow gets bad, the mountain may close."

Velma, Fred, and Daphne
hopped onto the ski lift.
"See you at the top!" said Daphne.
Then it was Shaggy and Scooby's turn.

7

"Oomph!" The bench crashed into them,
and they tumbled onto the seat.
"Going up!" said Shaggy.
The buddies glided over the trees to the top of the mountain.

8

"Time to get off, good buddy," Shaggy said. "Count to three, then we jump."

"Rokay," said Scooby. "Ron, roo . . ."

"Ree!" Scooby and Shaggy jumped off the ski lift.
"Wooooaaaaah!"

They slipped and slid and teetered and tottered off the path, and away from their friends. They couldn't stop.

Finally, they stumbled to a stop —
in front of another ski lodge.
"How about a rest?" said Shaggy.
"Reah!" said Scooby.
Shaggy grinned. "Groovy. We can get those hot dogs now!"

11

Inside, the lodge was dark. Cobwebs hung from the
ceiling. Sheets covered tables. And dust covered everything.

"There's no one here," said Shaggy, disappointed. "No cooks or waiters."
He picked up a phone. "And no dial tone. We can't even call for pizza."

Find the difference between Shaggy on this page and the one below.

"Rait!"

Scooby padded through swinging doors, into the kitchen.

He sniffed around the cabinets. "Rummy!"

Answer: missing pocket, scarf is orange and blue

"Yummy?" said Shaggy. He opened a door. Out tumbled popcorn, potato chips, and all sorts of food and drinks. "Eat first!" Shaggy shouted. "Ski later!"

Scooby ripped open one bag.

Shaggy ripped open another.

They began to eat.

C-r-e-a-k!

Shaggy stopped in the middle of biting a chip.

"What was that?"

C-R-E-A-K!
Slowly, slowly, the kitchen door swung open.
Slowly, slowly, the kitchen door swung closed.
"Whoooo!"
A ghostly cry filled the air.

Boom! Something crashed upstairs. Shaggy dropped his popcorn.
Scooby dropped his chips.

"Rhost!" shouted Scooby.

"Ghost!" shouted Shaggy.

Shapes swirled
outside the windows.
Bangs echoed through the lodge.
"Whoooo! Whoooo!"
"Like, it's not just one ghost!" Shaggy
moaned. "This place is crawling with ghosts!"

19

They ran for the door.

"Push!" said Shaggy. Scooby pushed. But the door wouldn't open.

"Rull!" Scooby said. Shaggy pulled. But the door still wouldn't open.

"We're trapped!" Shaggy cried.

They crawled under the table.

"Oh, why did we go off on our own?" Shaggy sobbed. "How are we going to get out?"

All at once, the door swung open. Great white shapes floated inside.

"Zoinks! They're closing in!" said Shaggy.

One lifted an arm and pointed right at them.

"Raggy!" shouted Scooby. "Run!"

SEEK & FIND

Find the shovel on this page, and then find four more on the following pages.

The buddies raced around the ghosts.

"Stop!" one commanded.

Shaggy skidded to a stop. The voice sounded familiar.

"What are you guys doing?" asked another ghost.

"Are you okay?" asked the third.

Answer on pages 25, 26, 27, 30

"Velma?" said Shaggy. "Fred?"

"Raphne?" Scooby added.

Velma, Daphne, and Fred shook off the snow covering their heads, arms, and legs.

"Of course it's us," said Fred. "We followed your tracks to find you."

"We thought you were ghosts," Shaggy explained, "and that this place is haunted."

Whooooo!
Whoooo! Boom! Crash!
Shaggy jumped into Scooby's arms.
"See?" said Shaggy. "Listen to that!"
"The wind is making the whooo noise," Velma said.
"And the booms?" asked Shaggy.

"That's just tree branches hitting the roof."

Shaggy pointed to the white shapes outside the window. "Explain that!"

Fred laughed. "Easy. It's snow blowing around."

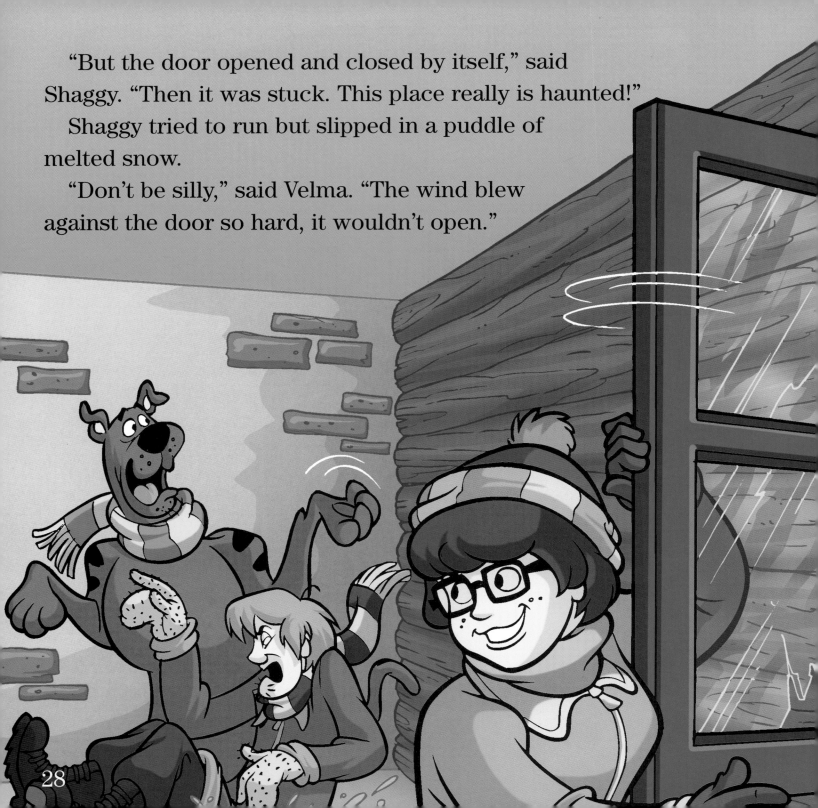

"But the door opened and closed by itself," said Shaggy. "Then it was stuck. This place really is haunted!"

Shaggy tried to run but slipped in a puddle of melted snow.

"Don't be silly," said Velma. "The wind blew against the door so hard, it wouldn't open."

Daphne patted Scooby. "The storm is really bad. The mountain is closing."

Fred checked his watch. "We missed the last ski lift run. What are we going to do now?"

MYSTERY MIX-UP?

Unscramble the letters to solve the word mysteries.

kigsni

nomaniut

wnso

gotsh

morst

Velma shrugged.

"We can build a fire and wait right here."

Scooby gulped. "Rere?"

"This place gives me the creeps, but okay," Shaggy said, and he walked away.

"Raggy!" shouted Scooby.

"Like, cool it, good buddy," said Shaggy.
He pointed to the fire. "I'm just getting the marshmallows!"

"See, guys, this ski lodge isn't so bad," said Velma.

"So long as we don't run out of marshmallows it's cool. Right, Scooby?" Shaggy replied.

"Scooby-Dooby Doo!"

Scooby-Doo!

Create your own bonus book!

Step 1:
Color both sides of this storybook page.

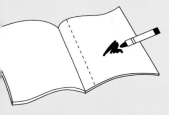

Step 2:
With an adult's supervision, carefully cut along the dotted line.

Step 3:
Repeat steps 1 and 2 in the first 12 books of the Scooby-Doo Read & Solve mystery series.

Please turn page over for further instructions.

"This place looks deserted," said Daphne. "Hey, gang!" said Shaggy. "Zeb musta gotten here before us!… But it looks like… gulp… the witch got to him!"

"This isn't Zeb, Shaggy," said Velma.
"I thought he, like, shrunk…" said Shaggy.
"No… It's a voodoo doll that looks like him—probably made by that witch."
"Time to go check out the swamp," announced Fred.

10

Step 4:
Put all 12 cut-out pages neatly in order.

Step 5:
Staple three times on the left side of the paper stack to create the book's spine.

Step 6:
Congratulations, you have solved the mystery!

You have now created your very own Scooby-Doo storybook!